Felicia Bond

Tumble Bumble

Front Street
Arden, North Carolina

Copyright © 1996 by Felicia Bond
All rights reserved
Library of Congress Cataloging-in-Publication Data
Bond, Felicia.
    Tumble bumble / [written and illustrated] by
Felicia Bond.
        p. cm.
    Summary: As a tiny bug walks along, he is joined
by a cat, a crocodile, a pig, and other animals, all of
which end up in a boy's bed.
    ISBN 1-886910-15-4 (alk. paper)
    [1. Animals — Fiction. 2. Stories in rhyme.] I. Title.
PZ8.3B615Tu   1996
[E] — dc20   96-14417
Printed in Hong Kong by Blaze I.P.I.
Type design by Susan M. Sherman
First edition

For Nina

A tiny bug went for a walk.
He met a cat and stopped to talk.

They fell in step and strolled a while,
and bumped into a crocodile.

The crocodile grinned wide with glee,

then introduced her friend the bee.

They all began to dance a jig
and bumped into a baby pig.

"Oink!" he squealed. "That was my tail!"
They apologized to no avail.

So the crocodile sang him a song,
and as she sang they bounced along.

Zigging, zagging down the road,
they bumped into a big green toad.

The startled toad then scared a mouse

who bumped into a yellow house.

They kissed his head, then rang the bell.
When no one came, they said, "Oh well . . ."

and tippy-toeing on fourteen feet,

they looked for something good to eat.

Tumble bumble up the stairs,

they opened doors and checked for bears.

In one room they found a bed.
"I'm really tired!" the crocodile said.

She stretched out long beside the bee.
The toad hopped in, which made them three.

Then came the cat, yawning big.

Behind him was the baby pig.
The bug came next, and last the mouse—

all squashed together in someone's house.

And this is where the bug's walk ends—

With eight . . .

No, nine! . . .

No, ten! . . . new friends.

HOORAY!